Ben's Rocket

by Anne Cassidy

Illustrated by Steve Cox

FRANKLIN WATTS
LONDON • SYDNEY

First published in 2015 by
Franklin Watts
338 Euston Road
London
NW1 3BH

Franklin Watts Australia
Level 17/207 Kent Street
Sydney
NSW 2000

A CIP catalogue record for this book is available
from the British Library.

ISBN 978 1 4451 3790 2 (hbk)
ISBN 978 1 4451 3793 3 (pbk)
ISBN 978 1 4451 3792 6 (library ebook)
ISBN 978 1 4451 3791 9 (ebook)

Series Editor: Jackie Hamley
Series Advisor: Catherine Glavina
Series Designer: Peter Scoulding

Printed in China

Franklin Watts is a division of
Hachette Children's Books,
an Hachette UK company.
www.hachette.co.uk

For Ben –
lots of love, A.C.

Ben wanted to
go into space.

He had a space suit.

5

He built a rocket.

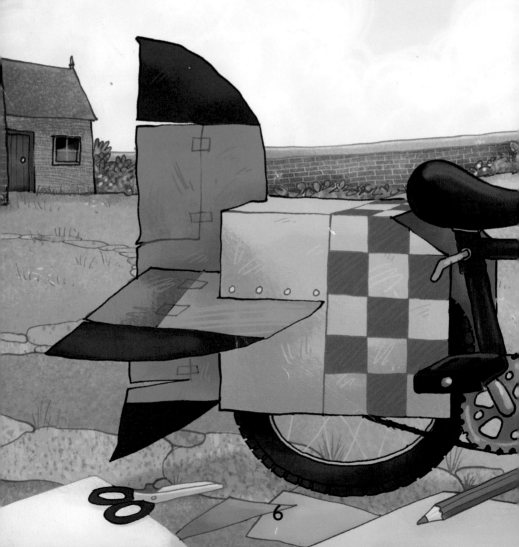

6

7

He tried to take off.

But he landed in
the sandpit.

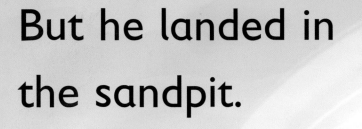

Ben got some balloons.

The balloons didn't take him high enough.

"I'll show you space,"
his dad said.

Ben looked through
the telescope.

"Wow!" he said.
"Look at those stars!"

Ben was happy.

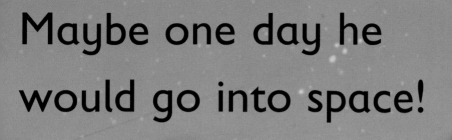

Maybe one day he would go into space!

Puzzle Time!

Put these pictures in the right order and tell the story!

shocked

happy

surprised

thrilled

Which words describe Ben when he crashes, and which when he sees space?

Turn over for answers!

Notes for adults

TADPOLES are structured to provide support for newly independent readers. The stories may also be used by adults for sharing with young children.

Starting to read alone can be daunting. TADPOLES help by providing visual support and repeating words and phrases. These books will both develop confidence and encourage reading and rereading for pleasure.

If you are reading this book with a child, here are a few suggestions:

1. Make reading fun! Choose a time to read when you and the child are relaxed and have time to share the story.
2. Talk about the story before you start reading. Look at the cover and the blurb. What might the story be about? Why might the child like it?
3. Encourage the child to employ a phonics first approach to tackling new words by sounding the words out.
4. Invite the child to retell the story, using the jumbled picture puzzle as a starting point. Extend vocabulary with the matching words to pictures puzzle.
5. Give praise! Remember that small mistakes need not always be corrected.

Answers

Here is the correct order:

1.b 2.f 3.e 4.d 5.a 6.c

Words to describe Ben when he crashes: shocked, surprised

Words to describe Ben when he sees space: happy, thrilled